IN MEMORY OF MY DAD, RON HEAPY, AND ALL HIS STORIES.
T.H.

FOR LUNA, WHOSE SOUL IS AS BRIGHT AND BEAUTIFUL
AS EVERY MOON THAT EVERY OWL SINGS TO.
I.B.

EGMONT
We bring stories to life

First published in Great Britain in 2020 by Egmont UK Limited
2 Minster Court, London EC3R 7BB
www.egmont.co.uk

Text copyright © Teresa Heapy 2020
Illustrations copyright © Izzy Burton 2020

Teresa Heapy and Izzy Burton have asserted their moral rights.

ISBN 978 1 4052 9288 7

70014/001

Printed in Italy

A CIP catalogue record for this title is available from the British Library.

THE WONDER TREE

TERESA HEAPY

ILLUSTRATED BY

IZZY BURTON

EGMONT

Little Owl and his mummy were both fast asleep
on their favourite branch of the tree where they lived.

But then something woke up Little Owl.

"Mummy!" he shrieked.
"Look! The leaves are all falling!"

Mummy tucked her soft wing around him.
"Little Owl, don't you worry. Now go back to sleep."

But Little Owl couldn't sleep.

"Mummy," he asked with a frown,
"won't our tree be cold without leaves?"

"Little Owl," said his mummy,
"let me tell you a wonder.

Our tree drinks
heat from the
Sun every day.

So when it gets
colder – and the
days shorter – our tree
sends leaves down
tumbling, as it soaks up
the last scrap of warmth
from each one."

"Our tree is BRILLIANT!" squeaked Little Owl.

"Yes! But now it's time for sleep,"
said Mummy.

But Little Owl really couldn't sleep.
"How does our tree drink, Mummy?"

"Little Owl," said Mummy,
"let me tell you a wonder.

Our tree has roots
plunging deep through brown earth,
stretching out,
twisting round and about.

These roots sink down further than you'd
ever think possible, with fine, tiny strands
that suck water from the earth."

"Our tree is AMAZING!" exclaimed Little Owl.
"It'll be here forever!"

Little Owl snuggled closer.
"Mummy," he said,
"can you tell me a story?"

"Little Owl," said Mummy,
"our tree's full of stories . . .

For, when I was little, I lived here . . .

. . . and my mummy and daddy did, too.

They left, long ago, but look –
their stories are still here . . .

in the rings of the tree . . .

. . . and the clasp of its roots, and the kiss of its leaves.

My parents felt the leaves fall,

just like you."

Above them,
the Moon floated high in the sky
with silver-struck stars
on invisible strings.

"Time to fly, Little Owl,"
said Mummy.

"But we'll be back, won't we?"
said Little Owl.

And then through the branches,
the owls heard the tree answer:
"I'll see you again with the sweet
morning dew."

And as they rose from their branch,
and the wind swept beneath them,
the owls sang back . . .

"Too-whit . . ."

". . . too-woOOOOOO!"